I remember Judy Pechet, 1924–2016 — BR

To Elouan, who was growing inside my
belly during the creation of this book — SK

Text copyright © 2019 by Bill Richardson
Illustrations copyright © 2019 by Slavka Kolesar
Published in Canada and the USA in 2019 by Groundwood Books

Groundwood Books / House of Anansi Press
groundwoodbooks.com

We gratefully acknowledge for their financial support of our publishing program the
Canada Council for the Arts, the Ontario Arts Council and the Government of Canada.

Canada Council **Conseil des Arts**
for the Arts **du Canada**

 ONTARIO ARTS COUNCIL
CONSEIL DES ARTS DE L'ONTARIO
an Ontario government agency
un organisme du gouvernement de l'Ontario

With the participation of the Government of Canada
Avec la participation du gouvernement du Canada | Canadä

Library and Archives Canada Cataloguing in Publication
Title: The promise basket / Bill Richardson ; pictures by Slavka Kolesar.
Names: Richardson, Bill, author. | Kolesar, Slavka. illustrator
Identifiers: Canadiana (print) 20189067330 | Canadiana (ebook) 20189067349 |
ISBN 9781773060897 (hardcover) | ISBN 9781773060903 (EPUB) |
ISBN 9781773062792 (Kindle)
Classification: LCC PS8585.I186 P76 2019 | DDC jC813/.54–dc23

The illustrations are in colored pencil, graphite, watercolor and gouache.
Design by Michael Solomon
Printed and bound in Malaysia

MIX
Paper from
responsible sources
FSC® C012700
www.fsc.org

The
Promise Basket

pictures by

BILL RICHARDSON   SLAVKA KOLESAR

Groundwood Books
House of Anansi Press
Toronto   Berkeley

When the world was just a little younger and
just a little sweeter than it is today, a mother
lived with her baby daughter in a room that was
smaller than small.

"A real mousehole," you would have said, and,
in fact, there was a mouse who lived there, too.

The mother didn't mind and the baby didn't
mind. The mouse went about her mouse business
quietly and professionally. The only time she ever
made a noise was when she was asleep and cried
out fearfully at nightmare cats.

They were poor, that mother and her baby, but the mother was determined that gifts would be given when gifts needed giving. She was proud. She was hopeful. She would find a way.

Where they lived was near the sea. On the day before her daughter's very first birthday, they went down to the beach. The mother looked and looked and looked some more until she found the prettiest and the pinkest of all the many wave-washed stones. She put it in her pocket.

On the way home, in an alleyway, by a trash bin, she saw a little basket. Whoever had thrown it away had not realized what it was. The mother knew. She knew right away.

"A Promise Basket," she said. "Exactly what I hoped to find."

She took that basket back to the smaller-than-small room, and she scrubbed it up till it was as good as nearly new. She found a dangle of ribbon and a scrap of paper good enough to use for wrapping, and good enough for writing on, too. She set to work.

And when the baby woke, on the morning of her first birthday, the Promise Basket was ready. All it contained was the pretty pink stone, tied up with the paper and ribbon.

When the stone was unwrapped and rosy in the morning sun, the mother read to her daughter what she'd written on the scrap of paper.

A stone when it's thrown can damage, can break,
but nothing can shatter the promise I make.
This stone and this promise are all I can give:
I'll love you each day for as long as I live.

And she kept her promise and the Promise Basket, too, and the stone and the promise in it.

December came. There, on Christmas morning, was the Promise Basket, hanging where a stocking might have been. Inside the basket, tied up with a scrap of paper and ribbon, was a stone, different from the first, but just as pretty — jet black, with a chalk-white stripe around the middle.

When the stone was unwrapped and glowing in the light of an angel candle, the mother read to her daughter what she'd written on the scrap of paper.

A stone when it's thrown can damage, can break,
but nothing can shatter the promise I make.
I'll wrap you in love, keep you safe, keep you warm.
I'll do what I'm able to guard you from harm.

And she kept her promise and the Promise Basket, too, and the stones and the promises in it.

And whenever a time came that a gift needed giving, her little girl (who didn't stay little for long) would find the basket and a pretty stone — amber or gray, honey-colored or obsidian — tied up with paper and ribbon.

When the little girl was a not-so-little girl, when she lost the last of her baby teeth, her mother wrote:

A stone when it's thrown can damage, can break,
but nothing can shatter the promise I make.
I'll love you, my girl, with your beautiful smile,
from minutes to hours, from inches to miles.

And she kept her promise and the Promise Basket, too, and the stones and the promises in it.

And on the day that not-so-little girl became a teenager, and when her mother saw how tall she'd grown, how strong, she wrote:

A stone when it's thrown can damage, can break,
but nothing can shatter the promise I make.
You're ready to fly, and I want you to know
I won't hold you back when it's time to let go.

And she kept her promise and the Promise Basket, too, and the stones and the promises in it.

And when that nearly grown-up girl was almost
a woman, and when she loved someone who
didn't love her back, her mother wrote:

A stone when it's thrown can damage, can break,
but nothing can shatter the promise I make.
Dark times might find us, but always they end.
I'm here and I love you and heartbreak will mend.

And she kept her promise and the Promise
Basket, too, and the stones and the promises in it.

She kept them all, basket and stones and promises, until the day her daughter's own daughter was born.

The mother went to the beach then. She looked and looked and looked some more until she found a stone that was pretty and pink and washed by the waves.

She found a dangle of ribbon and a scrap of paper good enough to use for wrapping, and good enough for writing on, too.

And when she went to meet her granddaughter for the very first time, she took that basket and all the stones and promises it contained. How heavy it was!

And when her daughter unwrapped the stone — so pretty, so pink — and when she looked at the scrap of paper to read what was written there and saw that it was blank, she smiled. She knew exactly what to do.

She took a pen and wrote:

A stone when it's thrown can damage, can break,
but nothing can shatter the promise I make.
One day you'll crawl, the next day you'll leap.
I promise you promises that I will keep.

And she kept her promise and the Promise
Basket, too, and the stones and the promises in it.